Rockets

HAUNTED MOUSE

Magenta and the Scary Ghosts

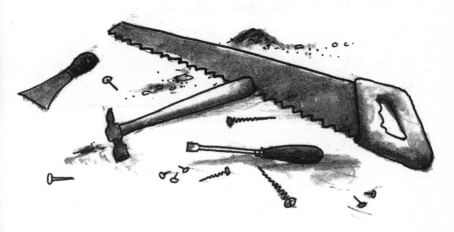

Dee Shulman

Rockets series:

CROOK CATCHERS - Karen Wallace & Judy Brown
HAUNTED MOUSE - Dee Shulman
LITTLE T - Frank Rodgers
MOTLEY'S CREW - Margaret Ryan &
Margaret Chamberlain
MR CROC - Frank Rodgers
MRS MAGIC - Wendy Smith
MY FUNNY FAMILY - Colin West
ROVER - Chris Powling & Scoular Anderson
SILLY SAUSAGE - Michaela Morgan & Dee Shulman
WIZARD'S BOY - Scoular Anderson

First paperback edition 2002
First published 2002 in hardback by A & C Black (Publishers) Ltd
37 Soho Square, London W1D 3QZ

Text and illustrations copyright © 2002 Dee Shulman

The right of Dee Shulman to be identified as author
and illustrator of this work has been asserted by her
in accordance with the Copyright, Designs and Patents Act 1988.

ISBN 0-7136-5977-7

A CIP catalogue record for this book is available
from the British Library.

Printed and bound by G. Z. Printek, Bilbao, Spain.

Chapter One

Magenta Mouse, who lived in the Haunted House, was having a lovely sit-down, when she heard a very strange sound.

It was hard to hear the strange sound because of all the other noise around the Haunted House.

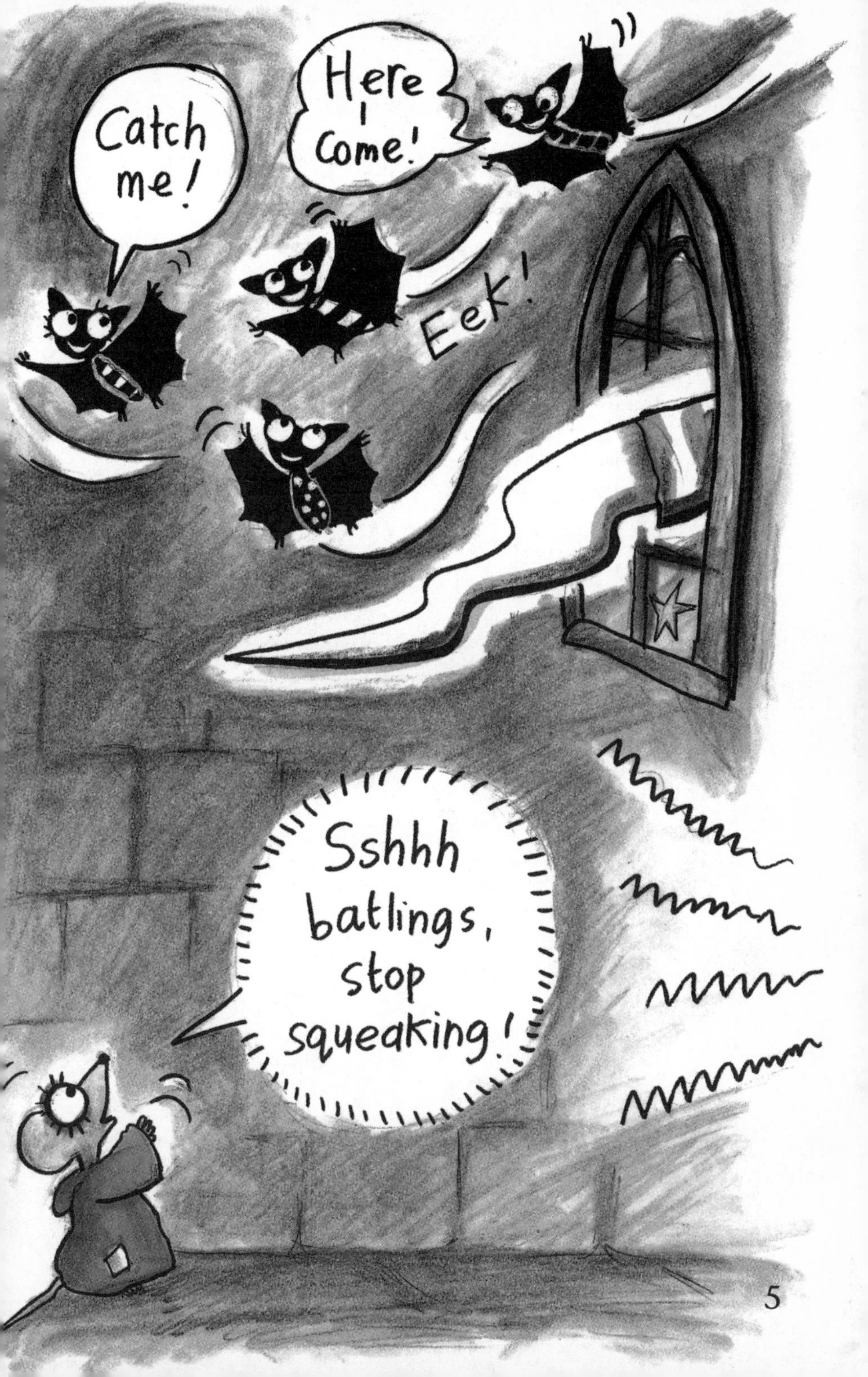
Catch me!
Here I come!
Eek!
Sshhh batlings, stop squeaking!

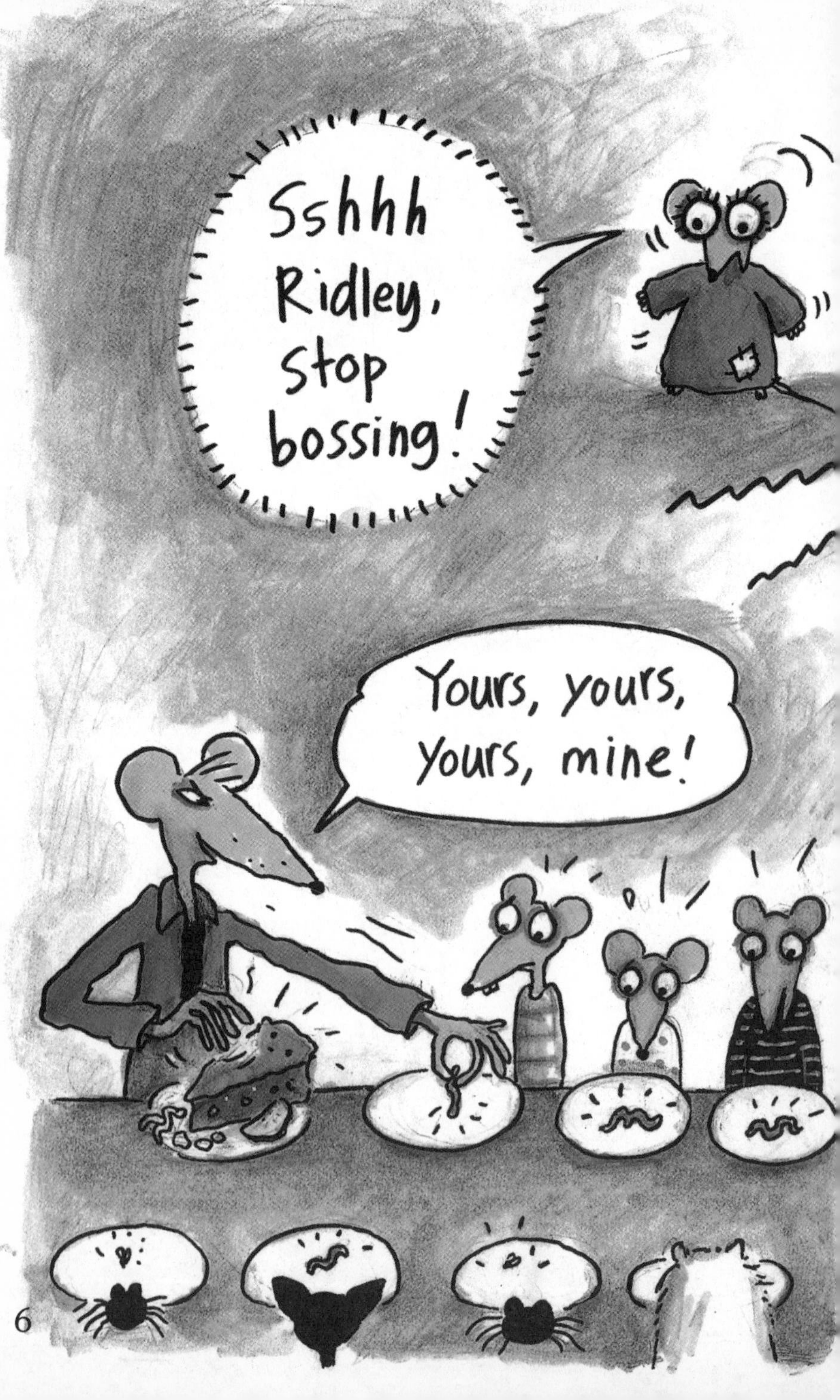
Sshhh Ridley, stop bossing!
Yours, yours, yours, mine!

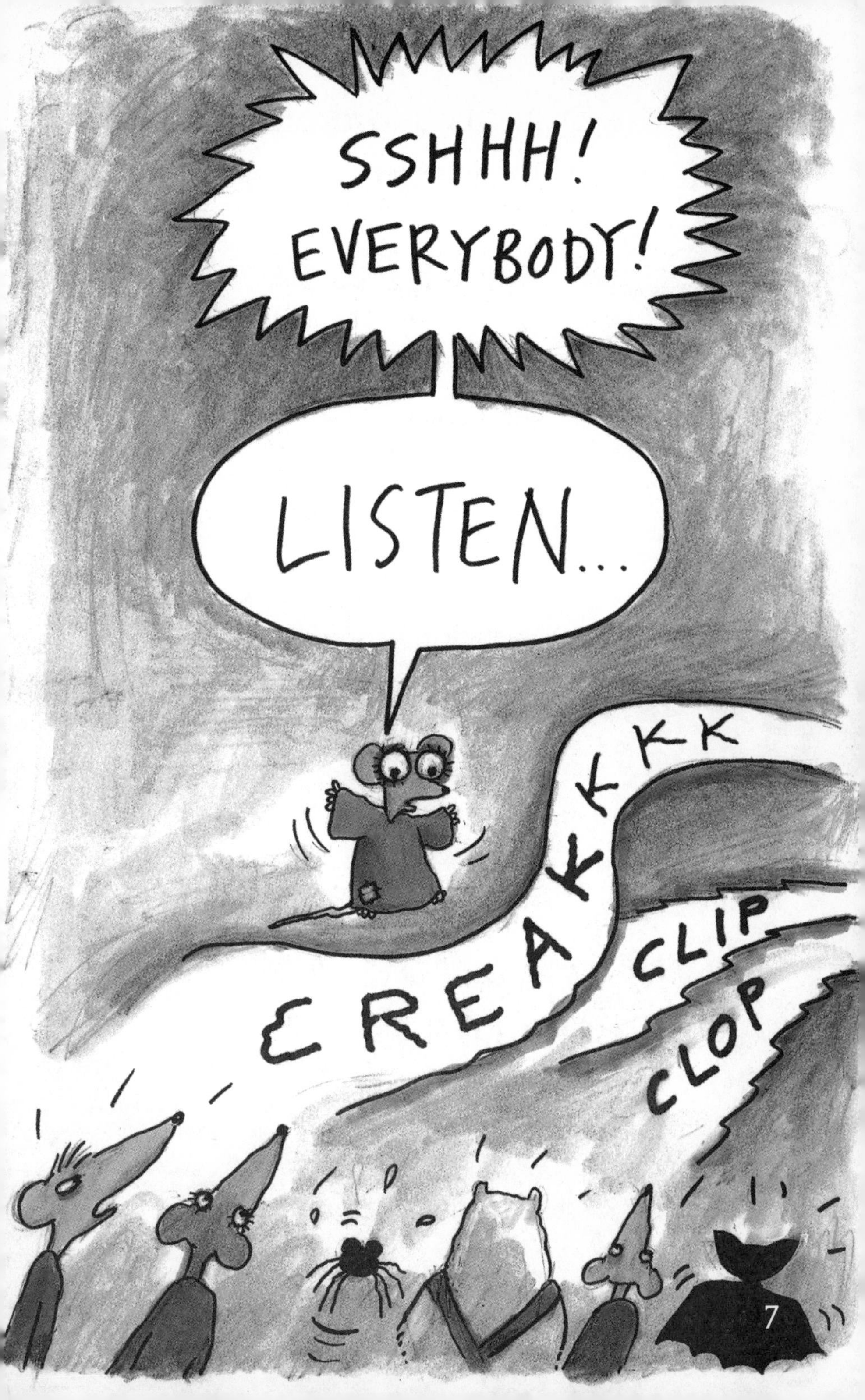
SSHHH! EVERYBODY!
LISTEN...
CREAKKKKK
CLIP
CLOP

What the animals heard made their fur (if they had any) stand up on end...

You see Baz, this **darling** house has so much space...

You are brilliant Jocasta! There's room here for at least twelve small flats. We'll make a **fortune!**

9

Chapter Two

The animals waited a few minutes and then came out of hiding.

What-shall we dooo-oo-ooo?

'We must think of a way to get rid of them!' said Magenta.

So they did.

'I know!' said Ridley, 'I'll lean against the front door and stop them getting in!'

The animals all looked at Magenta hopefully.

Magenta shook her head.

'Even you, Ridley,' she said, trying to flatter him, 'aren't quite big or strong enough to hold off Hooman Beens...'

The animals went back to thinking.

Oliver, the wisest owl, cleared his throat.
'The answer is simple. We will write a
sign on the door to say the house is ours,
not theirs!'

'But the Hoomans are so *big* and our
writing is so *small*...'

One by one the animals shook their heads, sadly.

The owls howled.

We're homeless!

The mice moaned.

We're doomed!

The bats bawled.

We've nowhere to go!

Everyone wailed.

We're all going to die! AAAGH!

'QUIET everyone!' squeaked Magenta crossly. 'How is a mouse to come up with a plan with all this moaning going on!'

Magenta sat in the middle of the room muttering softly to herself.

'Come on Godfrey, let's go and find Sir Boris right now.'

'Perfect!' said Magenta happily. 'The more ghosts the merrier! Let's go!'

It was a long way up to Sir Boris's attic, and as Magenta and Godfrey climbed, they were gradually joined by the rest of the animals.

Chapter Four

When they finally arrived at Sir Boris's door, Magenta knocked politely.

Inside the attic the ghosts heard
Magenta's tapping.

Sir Boris's posh voice rang out.

Felix echoed.

Young Jimmy should have known better.
Sir Boris smacked him across the back of
his head for being cheeky.

Magenta entered nervously, shadowed by an even more nervous Godfrey. The others all shivered behind the door.

Magenta coughed.

Sir Boris smiled smugly.

'Well, what can I do for you?'

'Oh, not another quarrel with the spiders?' Sir Boris smiled down at Magenta and tweaked her whiskers.

Not the Spiders, Sir Boris.

'It's not that rascal of a rat is it? He's probably due for a little haunting.'

Aagh!

Hee! Hee!

27

'No – it's not Ridley, Sir Boris. The thing is, Sir... the HOOMANS are here!'

'Sir Boris,' insisted Magenta, 'the Hoomans were here, and they are coming back on Monday with **BUILDERS**!'

The ghosts turned even whiter than usual.

'She said builders!' snapped Sir Boris, clipping Jimmy across the ear.

Joyfully Magenta joined the other animals outside Sir Boris's door.

Chapter Five

While all the animals scampered cheerfully back to bed, Sir Boris began sorting out the finer details.

What about you, Felix? Doing anything Monday, old boy?

Love to help out, Boris — but there's a bit of a party over at Agatha's place. Promised I'd be there...

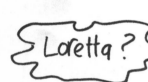

Loretta?

I've got a-a-a howling practice over at the Town Hall_

Oh well— Young Jim will have to do it. It's time you had a go at some real haunting...

B-B-But—can't you do it, Sir Boris?

Sadly not, old chap. I've got -er- work to catch up on... but you'll be fine.

So it was all down to Young Jimmy.

Chapter Six

Monday morning began quietly, and Magenta was just beginning to think that the humans had changed their minds, when she heard a huge roaring sound.

'Don't worry! The ghosts will save us...'
Magenta told the others, looking around
anxiously, 'They'll be here any minute!
Uh-oh! The Hoomans are *coming in*!'

Magenta was beginning to sweat.
Where were the ghosts?

Surely Sir Boris would come and scare
the builders away?

Magenta was just checking behind the curtains when she saw something that made her heart sink.

It wasn't long before the animals all knew the worst.

Suddenly Magenta grinned. The builders had just given her a great idea.

Chapter Seven

'Okay, what's this all about Magenta?' Ridley hissed impatiently.

But Magenta was tugging at the shabby old tablecloth, giving orders to the bats and the owls.

At last she got them into position, and then she started on the rats, the mice and the spiders...

We're making our own scary ghost! Owls and bats at the top- everyone else -HOLD ON!

Magenta was just rehearsing the owls on their scariest **WOOOOOOS** when the humans bustled in.

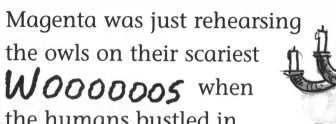

Probably get three good-sized rooms out of this one.

Stick a wall in there.

'Now!' squeaked Magenta and the tablecloth 'ghost' swooped down, the owls **WOO-oo-ing** as hard as they could.

WOO-ooo!

Look at that! The wind's caught that old tablecloth.

The animals were concentrating so hard on holding on to each other that none of them noticed what happened to the tablecloth...

But to the animals' surprise, the humans started screaming...

Within minutes all the humans had jumped into the trucks and bulldozers and zoomed away!

With a big sigh of relief, Magenta shut the front door.

Hiding behind it was...

Sir Boris!

Ah yes, Mouse— Here I am... er... to the rescue! Not too late I hope...

Hmphh!